KU-635-200

So every night, when bats
come out to play,

Bat would fly off in search of a friend.

He'd swoop from house to house across the forest. But the other animals were terrified when they saw his shadow.

"It's a monster!" squeaked the mice.

"Hide!" cried the squirrels.

Beattie the little bear peeped out nervously. "I bet the monster eats bears for breakfast!" she said.

We hope you enjoy this book.
Please return or renew it by the due date.
You can renew it at **www.norfolk.gov.uk/libraries**
or by using our free library app. Otherwise you can
phone **0344 800 8020** - please have your library
card and pin ready.
You can sign up for email reminders too.

NORFOLK COUNTY COUNCIL
LIBRARY AND INFORMATION SERVICE

NORFOLK ITEM

3 0129 08734 2219

HolcH

Deep in a forest, in a gnarly old oak tree,
lived a lonely little bat. The forest was
so dark, and his tree was so gnarly,
no one ever dared to visit him.

And Bat would fly home again, alone.

Back in his cosy home, Bat would cheer himself up
by baking. He just loved making delicious things
to eat. Night after night, he'd bake cakes and pies
and buns, for visitors that never came.

One autumn day,
the other animals were gathering
food for the winter. Everyone was
busy filling baskets with apples
and nuts and berries.

"I'm going to pick the most!" said Beattie. She grabbed the biggest basket and set off into the forest.

"Don't go too far," called the others. "Remember the monster!"

But Beattie was
already on
her way.

She picked **more**
and **more**,

and walked deeper
into the forest.

She didn't even notice that it
was getting dark. But then
she came to . . .

. . . the biggest, gnarliest old oak tree she'd ever seen! It was the perfect tree for a monster to live in. A monster who ate bears for breakfast!

In fact, she could smell cooking now!

Beattie was about to run, when she realised the monster's cooking smelled rather good. Fresh bread and apple pies! Her tummy rumbled, and she thought, "Perhaps I could just climb up and take a look?"

Bat was startled to hear a sound outside his house.
Did he have a visitor?

Then a huge furry paw reached through his window.
Bat squeaked in fear: "Eek!"

"The monster!"

cried Beattie,

and she

tumbled

down

with a

bump!

Then a voice called . . .

"Are you all right?" and a tiny
little bat fluttered over her head.
"I was running from the monster,"
said Beattie.

Bat sighed. "I wish they'd stop saying that about me. There isn't any monster. There's only me. No one ever wants to be my friend. They're all too scared."

"I'll be your friend!" said Beattie. She was wondering what they could play, when Bat asked,

"Do you like baking?"

Next morning, Beattie's friends were very worried. She'd been gone all night. What if she'd met the monster? They raced through the forest, following her paw prints.

"We're coming, Beattie!" they cried.

"We'll find you!"

"We'll save you!"

Suddenly they spotted Beattie's basket, and all the food she'd gathered. This must be the monster's house – and they could smell cooking!

"The monster's eating Beattie for breakfast!" cried the mice.

Fox banged on the door.
"Monster! Give us our friend back!"

Then everyone **howled** and **squeaked** and made
such a hullabaloo, they didn't hear the window open . . .

Out peeped Beattie's head.

"Beattie! You're safe!
We thought you'd met
the monster."

"I have," said Beattie. "In fact he's coming down right now to let you in." The animals gasped . . .

. . . and then laughed.
"That's not a monster,
**that's a tiny
little bat!**"

Bat looked at the crowd of animals and smiled. "I think we're going to need a lot more cake!"

So everyone crowded into Bat's house and together they baked . . .

and laughed . . .

. . . and Bat shared his best recipes.

That night, and many nights after,
the animals feasted by the beautiful,
gnarly old oak tree.

And they always loved to tell their favourite story – of the scary monster, the brave bear, and the friendly little bat who loved to bake.

For my parents, Dadi, and Joey

Published in the UK by Alison Green Books, 2022
An imprint of Scholastic
1 London Bridge, London SE1 9BA
Scholastic Ireland, 89E Lagan Road,
Dublin Industrial Estate, Glasnevin, Dublin D11 HP5F
www.scholastic.co.uk
Designed by Zoë Tucker

Text and illustrations copyright © Raahat Kaduji, 2022

Raahat Kaduji has asserted and reserved her moral rights
as the author and illustrator of this Work.

HB ISBN: 978 0 702312 85 4
PB ISBN: 978 0 702312 86 1

All rights reserved
Printed in Italy

Paper made from wood grown in responsible
and other controlled forest resources.

3 5 7 9 10 8 6 4 2

MIX
Paper from
responsible sources
FSC® C023419
FSC
www.fsc.org